For Ernestine and her girls and boys—Libby and Evan,

Katharine, Lauren, and Ryan —K.M.L.

For Charlie, Pat, Ben, and Carly, my faraway neighbors —E.S.

Text copyright © 2019 by Kerry Madden-Lunsford

Jacket art and interior illustrations copyright © 2019 by Emily Sutton

All rights reserved. Published in the United States by Schwartz & Wade Books,
an imprint of Random House Children's Books, a division of Penguin Random House LLC, New York.

Schwartz & Wade Books and the colophon are trademarks of Penguin Random House LLC.

Visit us on the Web! rhcbooks.com

Educators and librarians, for a variety of teaching tools, visit us at RHTeachersLibrarians.com

Library of Congress Cataloging-in-Publication Data
Names: Madden, Kerry, author. | Sutton, Emily, illustrator.
Title: Ernestine's milky way / by Kerry Madden-Lunsford ; illustrated by Emily Sutton.
Description: First edition. | New York : Schwartz & Wade Books, [2019]
Summary: In Maggie Valley, North Carolina, in the 1940s, Ernestine, who is five years old and a big girl,
carries fresh milk to needy neighbors through thickets, down paths, and over a barbed-wire fence, despite her fears.
Identifiers: LCCN 2018008798 | ISBN 978-1-5247-1484-0 (hardcover) | ISBN 978-1-5247-1485-7 (library binding) | ISBN 978-1-5247-1486-4 (ebook)
Subjects: | CYAC: Neighborliness—Fiction. | Courage—Fiction. | Maggie Valley (N.C.)—History—20th century—Fiction.
Classification: LCC PZ7.M2555 Ern 2019 | DDC [E]—dc23

The text of this book is set in Kepler Std.
The illustrations were rendered in ink and watercolor.
Book design by Rachael Cole

MANUFACTURED IN CHINA
2 4 6 8 10 9 7 5 3 1
First Edition

ERNESTINE'S MILKY WAY

By KERRY MADDEN~LUNSFORD
Illustrated by EMILY SUTTON

schwartz & wade books · new york

Deep in the hills and hollers of Maggie Valley, where the sun rose over an old rock house, lived Ernestine, her mama, and their cow, Ole Peg. Daddy was off in the war, so it was up to Mama and Ernestine to keep the farm running.

Every morning, Ernestine hollered out her window to the
Great Smoky Mountains, "I'm five years old and a big girl!"

Then, rain or shine, she and Mama would head off to
the barn to milk Ole Peg.

Later, Mama ladled the creamy milk into her
tea and drizzled it over Ernestine's oatmeal.

They kept the extra milk cold in mason jars
inside the gurgling springhouse off the kitchen.

At bedtime, when Mama heated milk on the old woodstove, she'd say to Ernestine, "I'm the Big Dipper, and you're the Little Dipper, and way over in Germany, Daddy sees the same stars we do up there in the Milky Way."

Then Mama would pat her big belly. "And maybe by the time Daddy comes home, the twins will already be crawling."

When even a drop of milk spilled, Mama said, "Why, look, it's our own Milky Way."

Then they'd cuddle under quilts, telling stories of stars, constellations, and wandering planets.

One day, Mama said, "Ernestine, I need you to do a job for me. Mrs. Mattie Ramsey, who rents the shanty house down yonder, needs milk for her children's breakfast. Their daddy's gone off to war too."

"You want me to carry Ole Peg's milk all the way to the Ramseys'?"

"I'd do it myself, darlin', but Dr. Fairchild says I've got to stick close to home with these babies coming."

Ernestine jumped on top of the milk pail and stuck her chest out. "I can do it, Mama."

"It won't be easy," Mama warned. "You'll have to walk through the thickets of crabapple and blackberry by the creek, down the path of prickly gooseberry and honeysuckle, past the vines of climbing bittersweet, into the valley of doghobble and devil's walking stick, and through the barbed-wire fence."

"I can do it, Mama," Ernestine repeated. She climbed down off the milk pail and whispered, "I'm five years old and a big girl."

But did Ernestine tremble a little when she spoke the words?

Next morning, Mama bundled Ernestine up in her blue coat and woolen scarf. She handed her two mason jars of milk with the lids screwed on tight. "See Venus shining up there?" she said. "That's the morning star. It'll light your path as the sun comes up."

And so Ernestine set off in the silent dawn beneath a lavender sky. She carried the jars in an old feed sack close to her heart while the mountains slept like giant elephants under a scattering of stars.

Just as Ernestine entered the thicket of crabapple and
blackberry, she heard a *snuffa-snuffa-snufflin'* along the path.
Could it be a lone wolf rustling up a breakfast of berries?

But it was only a family of sleepy skunks trundling
single file along the creek's edge on their way home for
an early-morning nap.

"I'm five years old and a big girl," said Ernestine, tightrope-walking across a gnarled log.

When Ernestine reached the path of prickly gooseberry and honeysuckle, she heard a fearsome *grunta-grunta-gruntin'* in the brush.

Could it be a passel of sleek panthers with glistening fangs?

But it was only a cluster of whistle-pigs rooting up
a snack of dandelions.

"I'm five years old and a big girl," called Ernestine,
stomping down a trail of crunchy acorns and witch hazel.

As the sky turned pink above the vines of climbing bittersweet, the
mockingbirds chirped. Soon Ernestine found herself in the valley of
green doghobble and devil's walking stick, where she heard a mighty
big something *scratcha-scratcha-scratchin'* up a tree.

Could it be a great black bear with claws sharp as swords?

But it was only a ring of baby raccoons practicing tree climbing with their mamas.

"I'm five years old and a big girl!" yelled Ernestine, ducking as she carefully climbed through the barbed-wire fence.

What a relief to feel the buttery
sunshine on her face . . .

but then one of the milk jars slipped from the
old feed sack and rolled down the path!

She watched it bounce, spin, and twirl as she chased after it, still holding the other jar close to her heart.

Over and over it went, pell-mell, down-down-down into the holler.

Ernestine scooted, stretched, and straddled to catch that runaway jar of milk.

But it vanished without a trace.

Mrs. Mattie Ramsey sat on the step rocking babies as Ernestine made her way up to her shanty, blinking back tears.

"Howdy, Ernestine," Mrs. Ramsey said. "You got something there, baby?"

Breathless, Ernestine held up one jar. "I brought you two jars of milk from our cow, Ole Peg. Only I dropped one. And now it's lost forever."

Ernestine tried not to sniffle as children kept appearing from every which way. An old lady called from a window, "Breakfast! Y'all kids get in here!"

Mrs. Ramsey answered, "Coming, Aunt Birdy." Then she turned to Ernestine. "Never mind, child. Please eat breakfast with us."

So Ernestine went into the kitchen with all the children, and they poured Ole Peg's milk on their steaming bowls of oatmeal.

Suddenly, the oldest boy, Jimmy, appeared in the doorway, holding up something muddy and covered with leaves. "Hey, y'all, look what I found in the creek."

And there was the other mason jar, which must have spun so fast down the mountain, landing with a plop in the icy water, that the milk had churned into butter.

Everybody cheered as they spread butter on slices of corn bread, and Aunt Birdy sang, "Lordy, I can't remember the last time I tasted real butter. Thank you, Ernestine. You're a big girl and a good neighbor."

When Ernestine arrived home with two empty mason jars, Mama kissed her head, hugged her tight, and said, "I'm proud of you, darlin'. You're my big girl."

And every day after that, Ernestine toted two
mason jars of Ole Peg's milk to the Ramsey family

through the thickets of crabapple
and blackberry,

down the path of prickly gooseberry
and honeysuckle,

past the vines of climbing bittersweet,

into the valley of doghobble and devil's walking stick,

and through the barbed-wire fence.

Because she was five years old and a big girl.
And that's what neighbors do.

Author's Note

My friend Ernestine Edwards Upchurch (1937–2017) was a lifelong resident of Maggie Valley, North Carolina, and she liked to say "I bloomed where I was planted." Ernestine loved telling stories about growing up in an old rock house built by her grandfather, and I was lucky enough to hear the one from her childhood that inspired this story, which happened around 1942. Ernestine was five years old when many men like her father were called away during World War II, so the women and children worked hard at home to help each other while the daddies were gone. I learned a lot about the forties and fifties from Ernestine, including what a springhouse was. Although her family had electricity, they didn't have a refrigerator. They did, however, have a springhouse, which Ernestine called "primitive refrigeration." The springhouse sat on a creek, and the icy mountain water flowed through it, keeping the milk and butter cold.

I then added some details from my imagination to turn Ernestine's story into a picture book, including what would happen to a mason jar filled with milk if it rolled all the way down the mountain and then got tossed around in a river. A friend of mine who grew up making butter taught me about shaking up a jar of milk until it turned to butter, and I knew that was the magic ingredient for the story. If you want to try making butter yourself, fill a mason jar halfway with whole milk or heavy cream and shake it up and down for about fifteen minutes. Pretty soon you'll find a lump of butter to spread on your corn bread.

Corn Bread Recipe

by Kathryn Tucker Windham

Ernestine would never have used sugar in corn bread because that would make it cake, and she always used a cast-iron skillet to make it a crunchy golden brown. Make sure to have an adult help you, because this recipe involves a very hot pan.

INGREDIENTS

1 egg

2 tbsp. vegetable oil, and more for the pan

2 cups self-rising cornmeal

1/3 cup buttermilk

Preheat oven to 450° F. Beat an egg in a bowl. Add 2 tablespoons of oil to the egg. Mix in 2 cups of self-rising cornmeal. Add 1/3 cup of buttermilk. Stir until the batter gets good and mushy. Pour oil to cover the bottom of a cast-iron skillet. Heat it to real hot in the oven. Remove it from the oven and pour the batter into the skillet, then put it back into the oven and bake it for thirty minutes. To give it an extra-crunchy top, turn the oven on broil for the last minute or two, and you'll have a skillet of golden-brown corn bread.